JAMES
in the House
of
Aunt Prudence

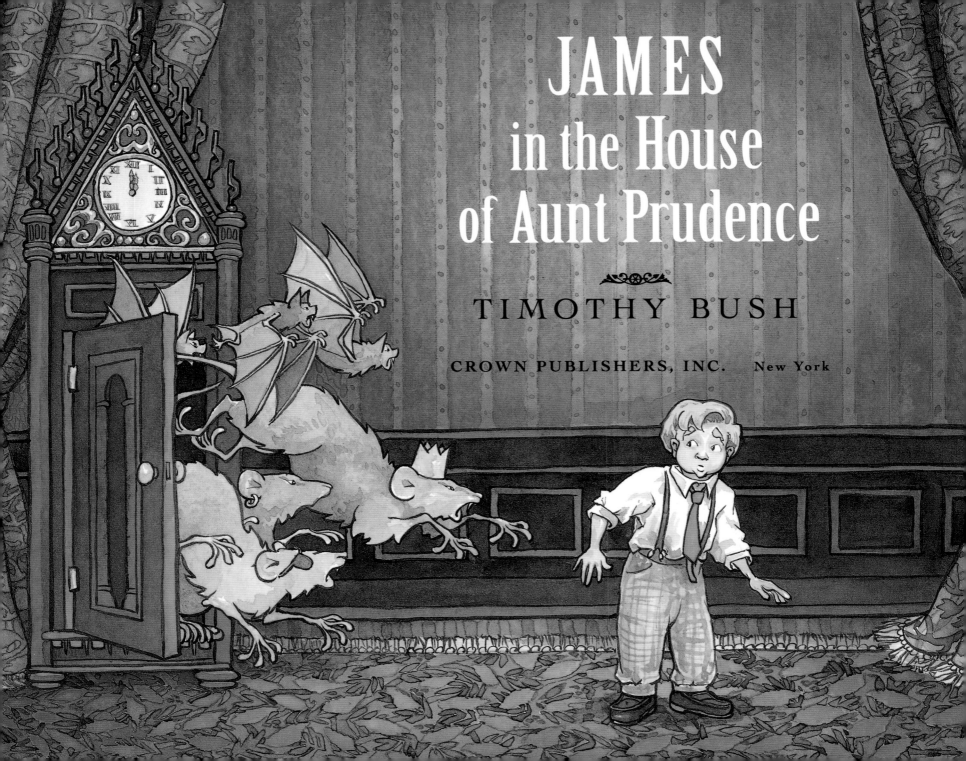

JAMES
in the House
of Aunt Prudence

TIMOTHY BUSH

CROWN PUBLISHERS, INC.   New York

To cousin Edward, who can take things apart and put them
back together with no parts left over

With thanks to the American Museum of Natural History and the Bronx Zoo
for leaving bears out where everyone can see them

Published by Crown Publishers, Inc., a Random House company,
201 East 50th Street, New York, New York 10022
CROWN is a trademark of Crown Publishers, Inc.
Manufactured in the United States of America
Library of Congress Cataloging-in-Publication Data
Bush, Timothy
James in the house of Aunt Prudence / by Timothy Bush.
p.   cm.
Summary: While visiting his great-aunt, a young boy spends the afternoon
being chased through the house by an assortment of creatures led by the
Mouse King.
[1. Great-aunts—Fiction. 2. Imagination—Fiction] I. Title.
3. victorian house
PZ7.B96545Jam   1993
[E]—dc20   92-40127
ISBN 0-517-58881-1 (trade)
0-517-58882-X (lib. bdg.)
10 9 8 7 6 5 4 3 2 1
FIRST EDITION

James was dropped off to spend
the day with his Great-Aunt Prudence.

Her house was elegant and filled
with Things that had been in the
family for years. James hoped
for a tour.

Instead, he was left with tea and macaroons while Aunt Prudence finished an important letter.

When the bear arrived, of course, there weren't enough macaroons to go around.

So they went to look for more.

The wicked Mouse King

had it in for the bear.

He attacked, and the
bear fought valiantly . . .

. . . but was torn to pieces.

James ran for his life, with the Mouse King and his confederates in hot pursuit.

They nearly had him when Aunt Prudence finished her letter.

"I leave you alone for five minutes and you stir up everything in the house," she said. "I suppose the bear's in pieces." James nodded, and they went back downstairs.

The tea was cold, so they made a fresh pot. "I should have expected it," said Aunt Prudence. "Your father was no better."

Then she played mazurkas at the piano while
James and the bear danced.

It would have been a perfect afternoon, but the Mouse King got into the kitchen and ate up all the macaroons.